The Dragonsitter's Party

First published in 2015 by
Andersen Press Limited
20 Vauxhall Bridge Road
London SW1V 2SA
www.andersenpress.co.uk

2 4 6 8 10 9 7 5 3

British Library Cataloguing in Publication Data available.

ISBN 978 1 78344 229 4

Printed and bound in Great Britain by
Clays Ltd, St Ives plc

MIX
Paper from
responsible sources
FSC® C018072

The Dragonsitter's Party

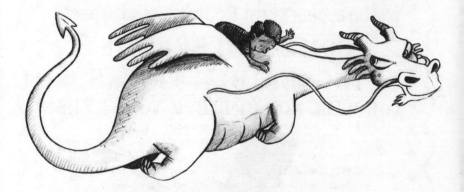

Josh Lacey

Illustrated by Garry Parsons

Andersen Press
London

Dear Uncle Morton

Did you get my invitation?

I just wanted to check because you're the only person who hasn't RSVPed.

I hope you can come. It's going to be a great party. We're having a magician.

Love from

your favourite nephew

Eddie

Dear Eddie

I would have loved to have come to your party. There is very little that I enjoy more than the work of a good magician.

Unfortunately I have already promised to stay in Scotland and help on the farm with Mr McDougall, who is a man short this weekend.

That man is, of course, our mutual friend Gordon, who is very excited about coming to see you. He talks about nothing else.

I can hardly believe that he only met your mother a few weeks ago. He already seems to know much more about her than I do, and I've known her for an entire lifetime.

Mr McDougall only agreed to give Gordon the weekend off if I would work in his place. It is the lambing season here and the farm has never been busier.

He will be bringing a small birthday surprise for you.

With love from

your affectionate uncle

Morton

Dear Uncle Morton

Thank you for the surprise. I can't wait to see what it is.

Mum is very excited about Gordon coming to visit. She keeps buying new dresses, then taking them back to the shop because they're not quite right.

I'm sorry you can't come to my party. I know my friends would like to meet you. Will you come next year instead?

I'll send you some pictures of Mister Mysterio sawing someone in half.

Apparently that's the best bit of his act.

I am going to suggest he does Emily.

She said, "That's not funny," and I said I wasn't trying to be funny. I just thought the house would be a bit more peaceful if I only had half a sister.

Love from

Eddie

Dear Uncle Morton

Gordon has arrived with your surprise.

Mum was definitely surprised, but not in a good way.

She said if she'd wanted your dragons to come and stay, she would have invited them.

She was hoping to spend some special time with Gordon this weekend, but she says their time isn't going to be very special if she's got to look after two dragons, not to mention the nineteen kids who will be descending on the house on Saturday afternoon.

Of course I was very happy to see them.

I can't believe how much Arthur has grown!

He's also getting quite good at flying. We put him in the garden in case he needed a poo after the long drive and he almost got over the wall.

It's lucky he didn't, because Mrs Kapelski was pruning her roses, and she has a weak heart.

I do wish Ziggy and Arthur could stay for my party. I know my friends would like to meet them.

But Mum said, "Not a chance, buster."

Could you come and get them ASAP?

Love from

Eddie

From: Edward Smith–Pickle

To: Morton Pickle

Date: Thursday 23 March

Subject: Dinner

Attachments: I don't do pets

Dear Uncle Morton

I just rang both your numbers, but there was no answer. Are you already on your way to collect the dragons?

I hope so, because Mum says they are living on borrowed time.

She and Gordon were meant to be going out for dinner in a posh French restaurant. Mum was wearing her best new dress and Gordon looked very nice in his suit.

But the babysitter took one look at Arthur and said, "I don't do pets."

We promised to lock Arthur upstairs in my bedroom with Ziggy, but she wouldn't change her mind, even when Mum offered to pay her double.

By that time it was too late to get another babysitter, so Mum had to cancel the reservation.

Luckily she had two steaks in the fridge, so they decided to stay here and have a nice romantic evening in front of the telly.

Unluckily she took the steaks out of the fridge, put them on the side and turned round to get the vegetables.

By the time she turned back again, Ziggy had eaten one steak and Arthur was half-way through the other.

So she's ordered a curry.

Gordon says he likes curry much more than French food, but I think he's just trying to be nice.

Please call us ASAP and tell us your ETA.

Eddie

PS If you don't know what ETA means, it means Estimated Time of Arrival.

Dear Uncle Morton

Arthur ate the curry.

I didn't actually see it happen because I was upstairs cleaning my teeth, but I heard the screams.

Mum says if you're not here first thing tomorrow morning, she's going to put your dragons on the train and send them back to Scotland on their own.

To be honest, I can understand why she's so upset.

She's been looking forward to her date with Gordon for ages and your dragons have just ruined it.

She won't even let them into the house.

She chased them onto the patio with a broom and says they have to stay there all night.

I wanted to stay with them in my sleeping bag, but Mum says I'll catch my death of cold.

I hope the dragons don't catch theirs.

Eddie

Dear Eddie

I'm terribly sorry I haven't replied to your recent messages, but it's all hands on deck for the lambing here.

Please tell your mother that I am very sorry. I had thought the dragons would be a nice birthday surprise for you. I didn't realise that they would spoil her weekend with Gordon.

Of course I shall come and collect them. I have just checked the timetables. If I leave my island at dawn and row to the mainland, I can get to the station in time for the first train and should be with you by the evening.

15

However, I have already promised my services to Mr McDougall for the entire weekend, so I can only leave him in the lurch if Gordon comes straight back here and does the lambing himself.

Unless your mother would prefer him to stay where he is?

Morton

PS Your mother is quite right: however warm your sleeping bag may be, you will be much more comfortable in your own bed. There is no need to be concerned about Ziggy and Arthur. They are used to Scottish winters and Outer Mongolian blizzards, so a short spell in the garden won't do them any harm.

From: Edward Smith–Pickle

To: Morton Pickle

Date: Friday 24 March

Subject: Gas

Attachments: Porridge

Dear Uncle Morton

I told Mum what you said. She thought about it for a bit. Then she said, "Fine."

I think she must really like Gordon.

Mum even let the dragons back inside.

I just hope the smell doesn't make her change her mind.

Arthur has been doing terrible farts all morning. The whole house stinks of curry.

He'd better stop before tomorrow or my friends will be poisoned.

Now they're having porridge for breakfast.

I wouldn't have thought dragons liked porridge, but yours seem to.

Gordon says no one could possibly resist proper porridge made by a real Scotsman.

Even I quite liked it, and I hate porridge.

I'd better go now. It's time for school.

I wish I could stay here and make cupcakes with Gordon.

But Mum says life isn't fair, even on the day before your birthday.

Love from

Eddie

PS Emily says can you send a picture of the lambs.

PPS Please say hello to Mr McDougall from me.

Dear Uncle Morton

Mum says thanks very much for ruining her one chance of happiness.

Gordon has gone for a walk. He said, "See you later," but Mum says he'll probably just drive straight back to Scotland.

I think they had a bit of a row.

It was Ziggy's fault. Or maybe Arthur's.

I don't know which of them bit the babysitter.

Mum found one who did pets. She booked another table at that French restaurant. She was wearing her second-favourite dress and Gordon was in his suit again.

Emily and I waved them goodbye on the doorstep.

Then we stayed here and watched telly with the babysitter.

Everything was going fine till she got hungry.

She should have known you never take popcorn from a dragon.

When the smoke cleared, the babysitter was jumping around on one leg, screaming at the top of her voice and looking for her phone.

Mum and Gordon had to come straight
home. They didn't even get to try their
starter.

Now Ziggy and Arthur are back on the patio.

They both look very sad.

They're staring through the glass, watching Mum eat their Maltesers.

She's going to put them on the train to Scotland if you're not here first thing tomorrow morning.

I don't like the idea of two dragons alone on the train, but Mum says they're old enough to look after themselves.

Please get here soon.

Eddie

Dear Eddie

You can tell your mother not to worry.
I have just booked a flight from Glasgow,
leaving at nine o'clock tomorrow morning.
I should be with you just after lunch.

I am very much looking forward to wishing
you happy birthday in person.

If your mother will allow me and the
dragons to stay for the afternoon, I shall
have a chance to see your magician in
action.

Unfortunately I appear to have mislaid your
invitation. Can you remind me what time
the party starts?

Finally – and most importantly – what would you like for your birthday? I'm ashamed to say that I have failed to buy you anything, but if you could give me a suggestion for the perfect gift, I shall try to find it at the airport.

Love from

your affectionate uncle

Morton

From: Edward Smith–Pickle

To: Morton Pickle

Date: Saturday 25 March

Subject: 3pm

Attachments: Opening my presents

Dear Uncle Morton

The party starts at 3 o'clock.

Please try to get here on time or you'll miss Mister Mysterio sawing someone in half.

I'm very pleased my friends will get to meet you.

Don't worry about not getting me a birthday present. Dad didn't either.

He didn't even send me a card. He just texted me this morning.

Mum said that was typical of him, which isn't actually true because last year he sent me a new bike.

27

I think he's just very busy at the moment rebuilding his castle.

If you would like to get me something, I would really like a magic set.

I did ask Mum for one, but she gave me a microscope and a book and another book and three pairs of socks instead.

Gordon gave me a fishing rod.

I always thought fishing was a bit boring, but he says nothing could be further from the truth.

He wanted to teach me this morning, but Mum said not when nineteen kids are arriving any minute.

They're not really arriving any minute. It's only ten past eight.

But we do have a lot of clearing up to do before the party starts, not to mention making the sandwiches, opening the bags of crisps and putting all the sausage rolls on plates.

So I'd better go.

See you later!

Love from

Eddie

From: Edward Smith–Pickle

To: Morton Pickle

Date: Saturday 25 March

Subject: My party

Attachments: Party pics

Dear Uncle Morton

Did you miss your flight?

You missed a great party too.

I thought it was great, anyway, although I'm not sure everyone did.

Mister Mysterio certainly didn't.

The problem was he didn't listen to me.

The first bit of his act went really well. First he made a coin disappear. Then he found it behind Emily's ear.

I said I could do that too.

Then he made ten coins disappear and he pulled a ten pound note out of Emily's nose.

He said, "Can you do that?"

I said I couldn't.

Then he asked me to pick a card, any card.

It was the Queen of Hearts.

He let me put the card back in the pack and shuffle them.

Then he took the pack and threw them in the air and just caught one of them – and it was the Queen of Hearts!

Then he made
a real goldfish
appear in a glass
of water.

Then he drank it
and the goldfish
appeared in
another glass.

Then he took off
his hat and put
his hand inside
and pulled out
a white rabbit.

I knew what would happen next. I had to warn Mister Mysterio. I shouted at him, "Put the rabbit back in the hat!"

"That's my next trick," he said. "First Henrietta is going to make some lettuce disappear."

He reached into his pocket and pulled out a handful of lettuce.

"*Bon appetit*, Henrietta," he said and gave the lettuce to the rabbit.

I shouted, "Look out! Behind you!"

Mister Mysterio just smiled. He said, "This is a magic show, not a pantomime. Let Henrietta eat her lettuce in peace."

She can't have taken more than a nibble before Ziggy swallowed her.

One gulp and she was gone.

For a moment, everyone was too surprised to speak.

Then Mister Mysterio went red in the face and started shouting at the top of his voice.

Mum said a self-respecting children's entertainer ought to be ashamed of himself for using language like that.

Mister Mysterio just shouted even louder.

He wanted Mum to pay eight hundred pounds to replace Henrietta.

Apparently it takes years to train a rabbit.

Emily said if he was such a good magician, why couldn't he magic the rabbit back again?

I thought that was actually quite a good suggestion, but Mister Mysterio took no notice.

He said if Mum didn't write him a cheque for eight hundred pounds plus his usual fee and expenses right now this minute he was going to call the police.

I think he really would have if Gordon hadn't taken him aside and had a few words.

I don't know what Gordon said, but Mister Mysterio went very quiet. He packed his suitcase and left without even saying goodbye.

I said maybe he could come back next year to saw Emily in half, and Mum said next year we're going to the cinema instead.

After that we should have had tea, but tea was cancelled because the dragons had eaten it.

The kitchen door was supposed to be kept shut at all times, but Mister Mysterio must have left it open when he collected his coat.

The dragons didn't leave anything, not even a single sausage roll.

Arthur even ate the candles from the top of the cake.

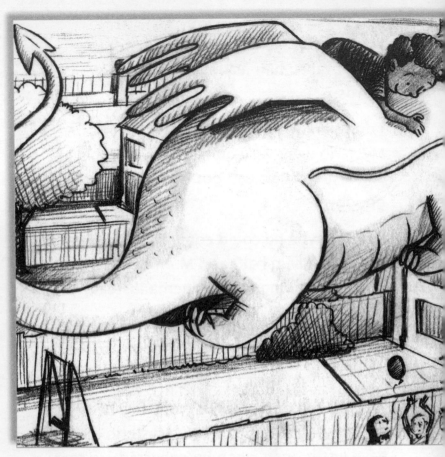

Luckily none of my friends minded, because
we went into the garden and Ziggy let us
take turns flying on her back.

Mum said please don't go too high or
someone will fall off and she'll never be able
to show her face in the playground again.

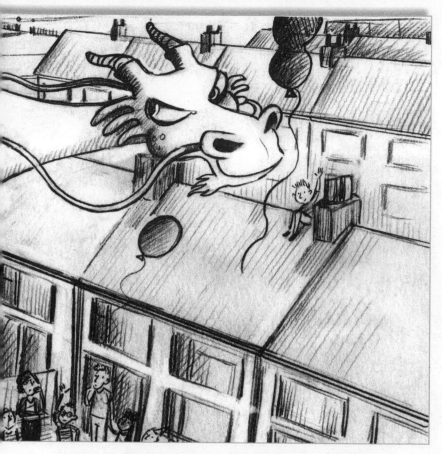

Ziggy took no notice. She flew my friend Sam to the roof of the house and left him there for twenty minutes while she was flying the rest of us around.

When Sam came down, he said it was the best birthday party ever.

I thought so too.

Love from

your one-year-older-than-yesterday
nephew

Eddie

From: Morton Pickle
To: Edward Smith–Pickle
Date: Saturday 25 March
Subject: Re: My party

Dear Eddie

You must imagine me clearing my throat and taking a deep breath, then bursting into song:

> *Happy birthday to you,*
> *Happy birthday to you,*
> *Happy birthday dear Eddie,*
> *Happy birthday to you!*

I am so sorry to have missed your party. We had a situation with one of the sheep last night, so it was impossible for me to catch my train to the airport this morning.

However, you will be glad to hear that her two lambs were delivered in perfect health just after nine o'clock this morning.

41

I have called them Eddie and Emily in your honour.

I have just looked at the trains and the flights. I could travel south tomorrow morning, but I would arrive at your house just as Gordon was leaving, which seems more than a little ridiculous. Would you mind looking after the dragons for one more night? Then he could bring them home in his car.

I have not forgotten your magic set, and I shall send it ASAP.

With much love and many happy returns

from your affectionate uncle

Morton

From: Edward Smith–Pickle

To: Morton Pickle

Date: Sunday 26 March

Subject: Magicians

Attachments: Hot bum

Dear Uncle Morton

I hope you haven't bought me a magic set for my birthday, because I don't want one after all.

I've decided I don't like magicians.

Today there was a knock at the door. It was Mister Mysterio.

He said he'd come for his money.

He kept shouting and waving his arms in the air.

Gordon said, "Why don't we calm down and talk about this like sensible people?"

Mister Mysterio said he'd had enough of talking. He just wanted his money.

Mum said he had to leave right now or she was going to call the police.

Mister Mysterio said he'd already done that himself, but they weren't interested. They told him that if he rang them with any more stories of rabbits and dragons, they would arrest him for wasting police time.

He said we'd have to sort this out between ourselves.

He said he wasn't going anywhere till we paid him.

He said he'd stay here all week if he had to.

He probably would have if Ziggy hadn't come to see what all the fuss was about.

That was when I realised Mister Mysterio wasn't a real magician.

A real magician would know it's not a good idea to shove a dragon.

For a moment, Ziggy stayed absolutely still.

All that moved was the smoke trickling out
of her nostrils.

Then she went wild.

Mister Mysterio ran down the street with
his bum on fire.

Gordon says he won't be coming back in a hurry.

Mum is worried he will, so she's asked Gordon to stay one more night.

She says can you carry on lambing?

Love from

Eddie

Dear Eddie

Please tell your mother that I am actually tremendously busy at the moment and can hardly spare any time away from my desk.

I should be preparing for my next trip abroad. I shall be travelling to Tibet to search for the yeti.

If Gordon is unable to return to Scotland tonight, I shall of course put my work aside and return to the lambs.

But I should be grateful if he could hurry home as soon as possible.

Morton

Dear Uncle Morton

You'll be glad to hear Gordon is loading his car now and his ETD is 8.15.

Mum is making him a Thermos of extra-strong coffee and some sandwiches.

I've made going-home bags for Ziggy and Arthur.

They've got chocolate buttons, gummy bears, cola bottles and lemon fizzes.

Gordon is going to drive all day. If the traffic isn't too bad, he and the dragons should be home in time for tea.

Love from

Eddie

PS If you don't know what ETD means, it means Estimated Time of Departure.

PPS Emily says please don't forget the photo of the lambs.

PPPS Your trip to Tibet sounds very interesting. Can I come too? I've always wanted to see a yeti.

PPPPS Have you ever read an email with so many PSs?

Dear Eddie

I'm very pleased to report that the dragons are safely back at home. As I write, Ziggy and Arthur are lying on the carpet at my feet, looking as happy as happy can be.

Junk food obviously suits them. I have rarely seen either of them looking so healthy. I shall have to ask Mrs McPherson in the Post Office to start stocking gummy bears.

Mr McDougall was delighted to see Gordon and sent him straight out to work in the fields. I believe he has delivered three lambs already.

I attach a picture for Emily.

You can tell her that these two lambs were helped into the world by her uncle and are now gambolling happily around Mr McDougall's fields.

For you, my dear nephew, I have put a small birthday present in the post. I'm sorry that it will be a couple of days late, but I hope you'll enjoy it anyway.

Thanks again for looking after the dragons so well.

With love from

your affectionate uncle

Morton

From: Edward Smith-Pickle

To: Morton Pickle

Date: Wednesday 29 March

Subject: Your parcel

Attachments: My best present

Dear Uncle Morton

Thank you for the egg!

It's my best birthday present.

In fact, I think it's my best present ever.

I know you said it probably won't hatch,
but I'm going to leave it in my sock drawer
anyway.

Then if a dragon does come out, it will be nice and cosy.

Please say hello to Ziggy and Arthur from me. I hope you're keeping them away from the lambs.

Emily says thank you for the picture and she has never seen anything so cute.

Mum is a bit sad. I think she's missing Gordon. If you see him, please ask him to come and see us again soon.

The dragons are invited too, of course.

Love from

Eddie

Barnacle, Mullet & Crabbe Solicitors

147 Lordship Lane, London EC1V 2AX
bcrabbe@barnaclemulletcrabbe.com

Thursday 30 March

Dear Mr Pickle

I have been instructed by my client, Barry Daniels, also known as The Amazing Mister Mysterio, to pursue a claim for damages against you and your pet or pets.

Our client was booked to perform a magic show at the birthday party of Edward Smith-Pickle on Saturday 25 March.

He had performed a little less than half of his usual routine when a creature, species unknown, pushed him aside and ate his rabbit, Henrietta.

Our client has been informed that the creature belongs to you and therefore you bear full responsibility for its actions and their consequences.

Our client will accept a minimum payment of eight hundred pounds for the loss of his rabbit.

Henrietta had undergone two years of intensive training and had assisted our client in more than seventy magic shows. His business has been severely disrupted by her loss.

Our client also wishes to be reimbursed for his full fee and expenses for the magic show.

Finally our client wishes to be reimbursed for one pair of brown trousers which were damaged in a fire caused by your pet or pets.

A bill is enclosed.

Our client would be grateful for payment of the full sum within seven days.

Yours sincerely

Bartholomew Crabbe

Senior Partner
Barnacle, Mullet and Crabbe

Dear Mr Crabbe

Thank you for your letter about your client, Barry Daniels, also known as The Amazing Mister Mysterio.

I was very sorry to hear about Henrietta and her unfortunate accident. As an animal-lover myself, I can appreciate how upsetting it must have been for your client.

I shall, of course, provide him with a replacement, although I would rather not pay eight hundred pounds. That does seem awfully expensive for a rabbit, however well-trained.

I have an abundance of rabbits on my island. They are always eating my lettuces. Mister Mysterio is welcome to take as many as he wants.

Perhaps he could teach me some magic at the same time.

I have spoken to my sister, who told me that she has already sent a cheque to Mr Daniels for his fee and expenses.

I suggested that she should only pay half his fee, since he only performed half his magic, but she has paid the full amount.

If I were Mr Daniels, I should think myself very lucky.

With all best wishes

Morton Pickle

The Dragonsitter
to the
Rescue

Josh Lacey
Illustrated by Garry Parsons

Dear Uncle Morton
I have to tell you some bad news. We have lost one of
your dragons. He's somewhere in London, but I don't
know where.

Sightseeing is the last thing on Eddie's mind when the
dragons escape on a trip to London. Will he find them
before they get into hot water?

Praise for *The Dragonsitter*:
'Josh Lacey's comic timing
is impeccable'
Books for Keeps

9781783443291   £4.99